The Pied Piper
of Hamelin

THE PIED PIPER
OF HAMELIN

Retold and illustrated by Donna Diamond

Holiday House • New York

Library of Congress Cataloging in Publication Data

Diamond, Donna.
The Pied Piper of Hamelin.

SUMMARY: The Pied Piper pipes the village free of
rats and when the villagers refuse to pay him for the
service, he pipes away their children too.
1. Pied Piper of Hamelin—Legends. 2. Legends—
Germany—Hameln. 3. Hameln—History—Juvenile
literature. [1. Pied Piper of Hamelin. 2. Folklore
—Germany. 3. Hameln—History—Fiction] I. Pied
Piper of Hamelin. II. Title.
PZ8.1.D567Pi   398.2′1′0943 [E]   80-12027
ISBN 0-8234-0415-3

For Duncan

A long time ago, there was a terrible problem in the town of Hamelin. There were rats everywhere, in every room of every house. Gray rats ran through the streets, brown ones danced in the doorways, and white ones jumped into the cupboards and stole the food. Old rats sat in the sun, and young rats played in the baker's bread dough. During the day, they dashed about the town. And at night, they leapt into the beds and curled up under the covers, so that no one in Hamelin could get any sleep.

The people of Hamelin were glum. They set traps to catch the rats. But the rats were clever and never got caught. They chased the rats with broomsticks. But the rats were fast and scurried away. They tried to scare the rats with loud noises. But the rats were stubborn and did not get frightened.

The people went to the Town Council, and each councilman made a speech. But that did not help. There was a meeting at the Town Hall, and everyone in the town made a speech. But that did not help either. Finally, they went to the Mayor

and said, "We've tried everything to get rid of these rats, but nothing works. What are you going to do?"

The Mayor shrugged his shoulders and muttered, "I don't know." He got up from his chair and stroked the fur border of his coat. Then he cleared his throat and made a speech. But the Mayor's speech did not help. No one knew how to get rid of the rats.

So the people of Hamelin went home, even more unhappy than before.

One day a stranger appeared in Hamelin. He was tall and thin and had large eyes as blue as the sea. His doublet was striped, his stockings were checked, and the toes of his shoes pointed up. Tied to his waist was a silver flute.

The townspeople stared at the stranger. They had never seen anyone in such colorful clothes. They whispered to each other as he walked to the Town Hall and entered the Mayor's office.

The stranger stood for a moment in the middle of the room.

"I am called the Pied Piper," he said.

The Mayor looked into the Pied Piper's deep blue eyes and then at the silver flute tied to his waist.

"I can do many things with charms and magic," the Piper continued. "If I rid your town of rats, will you pay me five hundred guilders?"

The Mayor sputtered, "Five hundred guilders is a lot of money."

The Pied Piper turned toward the door, but the Mayor called him back.

"Very well," the Mayor said. "If you can get rid of the rats, your fee will be paid."

The Pied Piper smiled. His blue eyes sparkled. Then he bowed to the Mayor and walked out of the room.

No one saw the Pied Piper again until evening. The sun was setting behind the houses and Hamelin was filled with shadows. The Piper stood in the market square and raised the silver flute to his lips. He began to play. The music was as sweet and gentle as the sound of water in a stream. It floated through the streets. The people left their houses to follow the

music. The Piper's song became gayer. Children gathered and started to skip around him. Then, the townspeople joined hands and began to dance in a big circle. They could not help themselves. The music had cast a spell that made them dance. They twirled until their faces were red and they could hardly catch their breath.

Suddenly, the Pied Piper took the flute from his lips. The
spell was broken. The people of Hamelin stopped dancing. The
children stared at the grown-ups, and the grown-ups stared at

each other. Then, as the moon rose, they went back home.

The Pied Piper tied the silver flute to a cord around his waist, and walked silently from the square.

The next morning, the Pied Piper returned to Hamelin. As he walked down the street, he raised the silver flute and again, began to play.

Soon, a squealing and scratching was heard all over Hamelin. Running from the alleys, scampering from the houses,

tumbling out the windows, rats came from everywhere to
follow the Pied Piper. He walked slowly toward the river
and, with each step, more rats gathered behind him. They
ran, they pushed, they tripped over each other as the Piper
played on.

When he came to the riverbank, the rats rushed by him and dove into the water. In a little while, all the rats had drowned, and the tune of the flute was the only sound that could be heard.

The people of Hamelin cheered and thumped each other on the back. They hoisted the Pied Piper onto their shoulders and marched through the streets. When they came to the Town Hall, the Piper jumped down and went to the Mayor.

"I have rid Hamelin of every rat. Now, will you please give me my five hundred guilders," the Piper said.

The Mayor stroked his chin and looked slyly at the Piper. "You play a simple tune on your flute and expect to be paid five hundred guilders? Any street musician could play your tunes. I offer you twenty guilders. That pays you handsomely for your work."

The Piper's blue eyes flashed. "You promised me five hundred guilders," he said.

The Mayor stamped his foot. "Twenty guilders! That's all you'll get. Take it and leave!"

"I will give you one day to change your mind," said the Pied Piper. "Do not disappoint me. You will regret it." And he walked away.

The next day, the Pied Piper returned and asked the Mayor
for the five hundred guilders he had been promised. But again
the Mayor refused.

"Very well," the Piper told the Mayor.

He stepped into the middle of the street and, once more,
lifted the flute to his lips. As he played, the people of Hamelin

heard the voices of children. Laughing and skipping, the children dropped their toys. Dancing and clapping, they ran out of the schoolhouse. Singing and giggling, they left their games to follow the Pied Piper. They came from every direction. Soon, all the children of Hamelin followed the Piper down the street.

The townspeople called to the children, but the children could not hear them. The music had filled their ears with promises of magic.

The Mayor gasped, the councilmen shouted, the parents pleaded, but the Pied Piper kept playing. Out of the town and down the road, the Piper led the children.

A short distance from Hamelin, there was a mountain with a pass made of large stones. The Pied Piper led the children to the mountain.

When the last child had walked through the pass, there
was a terrible roar. The earth shook, and the stones at the
entrance of the pass fell to the ground.

For weeks afterwards, the people of Hamelin gathered at
the mountainside and tried to clear the stones that blocked
the pass. But the entrance of the pass was never cleared, and

the Pied Piper and the children never returned. The children were glad to be in the Land of Promises. But without the children, Hamelin was never the same again.